THE LOUDEST ROAR

For Célia

Arthur A. Levine Books hardcover edition published by Arthur A. Levine Books, an imprint of Scholastic Press, March 2003

ISBN 0-439-57476-5

12 11 10 9 8 7 6 5 4 3 2 1 3 4 5 6 7 8/0

Printed in the U.S.A. 66

First Scholastic paperback printing, October 2003

THE LOUDEST ROAR

Thomas Taylor

SCHOLASTIC INC.
New York Toronto London Auckland Sydney
Mexico City New Delhi Hong Kong Buenos Aires

The jungle was a peaceful place.
Everyone was quiet. Everyone was calm.

Well, nearly everyone.

Clovis was a tiger.
Even though he was small, he knew
he was the fiercest, most roaringest tiger
in the whole world.

And Clovis
thought that
everyone else
should know
it too.

One day, he found some parrots
chatting politely as they
picked their juicy fruit.

Suddenly — there was Clov

He saw some muddy wildebeests
wallowing happily in their slimy swamp.

They didn't see the roaringest tiger
in the whole world.

ROO

Then, suddenly — there was Clovis!

The mighty elephants
were sunning themselves
peacefully at
the edge of
the jungle.

ROOA

Suddenly — there was Clovis!

“Oh, yes,” said Clovis proudly. “I’ve got the loudest roar in all the jungle.”

The animals began to complain. “Why should he spoil our peace?” squawked an angry parrot.

But what could they do?
Then a monkey, who was
very clever, had an idea.

Clovis didn't notice

the others

creeping up

on him.

Then,
suddenly . . .

OO
T
S
SQUAWK
OO

QUA
u oouu
UMPET
Toou
TRUM
SNAP
AP
SNAP
SNA
oouu

Clovis was
very surprised.

It was the
loudest
roar he had
ever heard.

The little monkey
looked up at the fiercest,
most roaringest tiger in the world.
"If you promise not to roar at us," he said,
"then we promise not to roar at you."
Clovis said he would try.

The jungle was a peaceful place.
Everyone was quiet. Everyone was calm.

And Clovis
was very well behaved . . .

. . . most of the time.